A HALLOWEEN NIGHT CAPER

ROBIN HOLLO

A Halloween Night Caper

© 2021, Robin Hollo.

Print ISBN: 978-1-09839-5-124

eBook ISBN: 978-1-09839-5-131

This is dedicated to my mother, Rose.

She has guided me and allowed me to become whomever I chose to be throughout my life. She created a childhood full of creativity, laughter, and precious memories.

But most of all, she has loved me unconditionally as I do her.

Not too long ago, in a quiet little town, there was an old woman who lived all alone in her secluded home on the hill. There were many rumors about her. It was said that she disliked the town and all the people who lived there. So anytime she would venture into town, people scattered like mice to avoid her! Children looked away out of the fear that after one look into her eyes, they would never be the same again. Mr. Walters, the postman, once told a group of boys at the elementary school that he would shake in his boots with fear when- ever he had to deliver mail to her house. She spent her days alone in the big, dilapidated house that time had decayed almost as evilly as her disposition. She would spend the better part of the morning traipsing through the old house, collecting magical trinkets that she would later bury in her gardens to ward off intruders. There were even some who said that the house was built on a graveyard and hexed by her ancestors so nothing would grow there. Yes, this is what was whis- pered in the halls of the schools and at the women's charity functions. This is what they said.

Many rumors and stories were told of the old woman on the hill. The townspeople feared her, especially the children. The fright- ful nature of the old woman and the eerie stories about her and her house held them all in a fear of what went on up in that house on the hill. The neighborhood children wondered how she survived alone. Had she inherited money from a rich ancestor? Perhaps she had murdered a wealthy husband. Not much was known, nor were any of them certain where she came from. It seemed like she had been there forever, never changing or aging, always the same ageless old woman in that weird old house.

The fact that no one had ever seen her in anything but black drew more concern and even rumors that perhaps she was a witch! She was known to walk with her head tucked down low and her eyes glistened through slits like black crystals glimmering in the moonlight. None of the children dared to come close, especially during Halloween! But then, one day a small group of kids made a decision that would change that. It was the kind of decision that comes after a few brave comments and a dare that no self-respecting kid could ever go back on. And so, it came to be that this group of friends would take it upon themselves to seek out the mysterious dark ways of the old woman known as Ms. Cruthers.

The elementary school was filled with kids screaming and running through the halls as the lunch bell rang. There was not only a chill in the air, but also excitement! At the end of the day, it would be the weekend and not any weekend, this weekend, it was Halloween! Pranks were already being pulled on teachers and on friends' lockers as the big day grew closer. Everyone was busy talking about Halloween parties, costumes, and the best houses to trick or treat at. Kids in heavy sweaters, jean jackets, and untied sneakers rummaged through lockers to grab lunch bags and dispose of books before heading to the cafeteria. The cafeteria was filled with the smells and sights of autumn. Walls were filled with pumpkins, skeletons, black cats, and witches while black and orange streamers were artfully strewn about the room and fluttered and flapped as kids ran by. In the corner was a stack of hay bales with carved pumpkins that had become ground zero for quick selfies with friends. Long metal tables with matching benches attached to them lined the room and would soon be filled with groups of friends catching up between classes as they scarfed down the carefully made lunches their parents provided and planned out parties and trick or treating routes that would garner the most candy!

Robert was always the first to arrive. He kept his lunch and books and, most importantly, his sketch pads in his backpack to avoid wasting precious time going to his locker. Robert was 11 years old. He was a small kid at four feet tall, very slender with light black skin, and he liked to keep his head shaved smooth. He wore jeans and a burnt orange sweater that his sister had given him for his birthday that year. He would never admit it to her, but it was his favorite sweater. Robert cracked then wiggled his thin deft finger. These were the fingers that created his anime characters like magic! His only real passion in life was bringing his characters to life in his sketchbooks; he was an artist. One day, he thought, he would be a famous artist, and wouldn't that old principal Miller be sorry he kept him back a year when he was famous! Robert dropped his bag on the metal bench and pulled out his sketch pad and colored pencils, laying them all out neatly like a rainbow. Then he pulled out a slightly crushed sandwich and placed it next to the pad without opening it. He had precious little time to work on his latest sketch, and the buildings needed more definition. He picked up a charcoal grey pencil and began shading the base of one of the buildings. It wasn't long before Kevin joined him, his curly brown locks of hair tossing about his soft brown, yet ever-cheerful face. Kevin was a year younger than Robert but about four inches taller. Kevin was slim and always wore pale blue jeans and some form of T-shirt with movie characters on it. Kevin was considered the leader of the group of friends. He loved a challenge and was always looking for the next adventure for them all. He loved a good mystery and was a dreamer at heart. He was fluent in his native tongue as well as English and little by little was teaching his friends too. Kevin strolled up to the table and dropped his lunch bag down. "*Hola*, my friend!" he said cheerfully to Robert as he carefully sat next to his friend so as not to bump his arm. Robert glanced up and grinned. "Hey how was art class today?" he asked. Kevin rolled his eye then laughed. "Not as good as it would be if *you* took the class!" Robert looked back at his work saying, "I told you, I can teach you if you want." Kevin opened his lunch bag, pulling out a crumpled PB&J sandwich and a pear. He frowned at the pear and put it back in the bag and opened the wrappings of the sandwich. "Nah I would never be as good as you; I'll just wing it." Kevin replied and took a bite of his sandwich. The boys sat in silence only a moment or two before two others appeared in the doorway. Kevin nodded to them as he caught their eye, and they headed over to the table.

"So, is Pluto a planet or not at this point?" Peter asked with his usual annoyance for life. Kevin shook his head and laughed as his two friends joined the table. Peter was 11 years old and was a bit of a loner but still managed to be best friends with Carl. Peter was a bit dark and often broody at times. His five-foot three-inch frame was always in a pair of black jeans and a black hoodie in hopes that it would help conceal his straight blonde hair and vivid blue eyes. All it managed to achieve was make the girls giggle and wiggle their fingers in a dorky little wave as they passed by. "You hate it now" his mother would say, "but soon enough there'll be girls all over this house!" Peter shivered inwardly at the thought and pulled out a couple of slices of cold pizza strips from his bag. "Well, NASA says it's a planet, so it's a planet," Carl stated as he dropped his bag down. Peter rolled his eyes as he opened his pizza. It didn't faze Carl, they had been friends for a long time, and nothing came between them, *ever*. "Hey, I'm going to go grab milk boxes who wants one?" Carl asked the group. Hands dug into pockets, and book bags and dollar bills were quickly tossed his way. Carl made a mental note of who gave what, so he could return the exact change. He was a bit of a math and science geek and enjoyed helping his friends with anything to do with math and/or science. Everyone seemed to have a special skill, except Peter, he thought to himself. Carl was of average height but already very athletic, thanks to the early morning runs and workouts with his dad, the town's sheriff. Carl was 10 but quite mature for his age with coily black hair and mocha-colored skin. Most days he too was in jeans, and today he was sporting his favorite sweatshirt that his dad had brought back for him from a trip to NASA. Carl headed off to grab milk and decided to grab five since he knew it would not be long before Marcy showed up. It was weird letting a girl be part of their group, but as girls went, she was pretty cool, and not all pink and fluffy like other girls. She was more like them and knew how to have fun and just hang out.

By the time Carl got back to the table, Marcy had arrived. Marcy was just over five feet and wore jeans and sneakers with a blue sweater. Her strawberry blonde hair was in a ponytail and tucked under a ball cap to help conceal the beauty she really was. She didn't like attention to her looks; she just wanted to fit in and have some laughs with the guys. Marcy was a multitasker, and as she made her way to the table; she had half her sandwich eaten already. Her backpack was bursting at the seams with homework, ideas, and lists. She was one of those people that saw everything and knew all kinds of cool stuff. The guys would often kid her about having eyes in the back of her head. Carl threw her a milk box, and she caught it with one hand, then grinned. Marcy loved baseball and was signing up for the boys' team again this year, even if they did tell her no, again. "Nice catch!" Carl said as he dropped the rest of the cartons on the table and passed out straws. None of them really used the straws other than to shoot the paper off the end at each other with a puff of air. The goal was to catch someone in the forehead at the very least! The straw wrapper shooting commenced, and soon wrappers were left strewn across the table, and sandwiches picked up and milks popped open. They made quick work of their lunches for this was precious time to catch up!

Marcy looked about at the boys; her sandwich was just leftover crusts by now. "Hey did you hear?" She began as she lowered her voice and crowded closer. The boys all scooted in a little closer, all eyes on her now. Even Robert looked up from his artwork. Being satisfied she had everyone's attention, she continued. "old lady Cruthers hasn't been seen in town in over THREE days!" She said as she watched for reactions. Carl shrugged and said, "Maybe she went to visit some family." He suggested. He didn't like to buy into all the rumors of the old lady. He firmly believed it could all be explained away like his dad told him it could. "Maybe" Peter began coolly, "she died up there and is going to haunt your dreams on Halloween night!" Marcy stifled a giggle; she knew how the boys hated giggling. "Maybe she moved into your basement Peter!" Kevin joked. Peter made a face and Marcy grinned. She liked Peter's darker side and egged him on. "What do you know, Kevin? You'd run screaming for your mother if she came up to you!" Peter laughed and Kevin scoffed and said, "Like you'd ever get close to that house!" It was tough to rattle Kevin, but she had. Marcy sat back, looking indifferent at him. "I'd go up there anytime; I bet Carl and Pete would go too." Carl and Peter looked at each other as if telepathically communicating and both smiled. "Yeah" Peter said, "I'd go in a heartbeat. I'm not scared of that old lady." Carl looked thoughtful and then said, "I'd go. There's always a logical explanation for everything." He stated. Robert laughed and said, "Yeah, she's a witch and is just lying in waiting for you all!" he said with a spooky voice as he wiggled his fingers at them all with a grin. Marcy moved a bit close, her expression more intense now with Robert adding to the conversation. "Yeah?" she began. "Well, I dare you to go up there " she paused for effect. "on Halloween night," she added. The group got quiet, and all eyes were on Robert. Unlike Kevin, Robert did not rattle easily. If anything, he remained even cooler under pressure.

Robert carefully placed his colored pencil back in its place and stared back at Marcy flatly. "And just what do you plan on doing when you get up there? Pick flowers?" His cool even tone hung in the air, and Kevin grinned. He was smooth, and when Robert talked, they all listened mostly since he didn't talk much! Kevin went on to speak, and Robert put a hand on his friend's arm. Then Robert leaned in toward Marcy. "I double dare you to come with me and prank her house," Robert replied. Everyone's eyes lit up except Carl's. "Hey, let's not go getting in trouble." Carl began. "Remember who my dad is! I'll get grounded till my next life!" But quicker than anyone could say old lady Cruthers Peter stood up and extended his arm into the middle of the group with his palm down. "Everyone who's not scared..." he began and cast a glance at Carl. Marcy slapped her palm down on top of Peter's hand with a quick snap. "I'm IN!" she said staring straight at Robert. Robert extended his arm and placed his palm on top of Marcy's hand. "In," he said flatly. Kevin followed suit "In!" he said. They all looked at Carl now and waited. Carl fought with the idea a moment longer before giving in to his friends. "Alright I'm in," he said as he reluctantly dropped his palm down onto the backside of Kevin's hand. Seconds later, all hands were flung up in the air by Peter's bottom hand, and they all called out in unison "Done!" just in time for the lunch bell to ring and classes to resume. They all scrambled to pick up unfinished lunches, their minds refocusing on what class was next. "Hey!" yelled Marcy before they all were gone. "We're going to need a plan," and they all agreed. Kevin looked at the clock as the second bell rang. "I gotta go! Let's just meet at the field after school!" he yelled as everyone began running in earnest for their next class, his pear tossed into the trash bin on the way out.

No one got much work done in the final class that day. Marcy and Peter were excited and already planning out the pranks they would play on old Ms. Cruthers, while Kevin and Robert felt a little like they'd been backed into a corner, and it would be their social demise if they caved now. "Who thought a girl would want to prank a haunted house?" Kevin said to Robert as they ran to class together. "That's what happens when you let a GIRL join the group," Robert complained. They both stewed on it for the rest of the day. Carl, on the other hand, was trying to find a different plan. A plan to get out of this altogether. He knew all too well what would happen if he were caught and his father would not only be angry, but worse, disappointed in him. He could almost hear him now. "We don't follow the crowd; we do what's right!" his father would boom. Carl didn't want to disappoint his friends or his dad. Maybe he could find a happy medium between now and Halloween. "Carl!" the teacher repeated. "Is it 'There', 'They're', or 'Their'?" she asked as she pointed to the sentence on the board. Carl sat up straighter and read the sentence. "It's 'They're' ma'am. They're going on a trip this week." He said with an ironic sigh. The teacher smiled brightly at him. "Nicely done, Carl," she remarked, and she continued with the lesson. *Yeah* thought Carl, *nicely done indeed!* and he sulked back down in his seat. He glanced at a picture of a hissing witch and cat on a broom that was on the wall at the front of the room and grinned a little. *It could be fun*, he thought. And slowly, Carl began to let go of the idea of not going with the others, and his mind, like the others, started to wonder and think about all the things they could do.

The final bell rang for the day, and the school emptied quickly except for the five of them. Instead of hurrying home to do homework or chores before dinner, they all met up at the ball field to talk about their plan to prank Ms. Cruthers. Carl and Peter met up with Marcy first. Marcy had drawn a few rough sketches, and the beginnings of a list were scribbled on a folder sheet of paper she held fast in her grip. "My mom was talking to Miss Everett the other day, and she was telling my mom that old lady Cruthers was buying all these candles at the hardware store." Marcy recalled the conversation to her friends. "They couldn't figure what she needed THAT many candles for, but I figure it's for spells and stuff!" Marcy stated plainly. Carl raised a brow in question. "Do you really think she's a witch?" Carl asked. "How else do you explain all the weird stuff that goes on up there?" Peter asked. "My dog went missing last week, and no one's seen him. I think she took him." Peter nodded in the direction of the house far off in the distance. Marcy and Carl nodded knowingly. "This girl, Jenny, in my homeroom said her brother saw her burying something in a big bag in the yard late one night," Marcy said as they sat on the bleachers. Kevin and Robert strolled up and sat with them. "She never talks to anyone either. Robert's mom said 'Hi' to her, and she just kept walking by and ignored her," Kevin said. "Yeah, you have to wonder why she doesn't talk to anyone and hides up in that old house all day. What do you think she does up there all day anyway?" Robert added. Marcy pulled out her sketch and list. "Well, we are about to find out." The sheer excitement of it all almost made Marcy squeak. Her sketch looked like a sad football field with stick figures with everyone's name next to them, and Robert rolled his eyes at the sight of it. Marcy stuck her tongue out at him. "We're not all artists, Robert!" she said. He shrugged, and they all pulled closer around the paper. "Ok, so what do you all think we should do?" Kevin asked. None of them had ever done anything like this before. Carl grinned. "How about we toilet paper the trees?" Carl had reasoned out that toilet paper didn't really do much harm and couldn't get him in too much trouble. Everyone nodded and grinned. "Yeah ... that's good," Kevin said. "Hey, what about shaving cream?" Marcy said with excitement as she made little notes on the paper. "Oh yeah! Shaving cream, that's awesome!" Robert said. Peter draped an arm over Kevin's shoulder with an evil grin on his face. "What about" Peter began with a cool mischievous tone, "eggs?" The group cheered in unison "Yes!" "Eggs!" "That's the best!" they called out. Carl felt a flicker of doubt.

"You mean, raw eggs?" he asked. Peter laughed out loud and shoved him "Of course, you spaz!" He teased. "You gonna hard boil them? Fry them?" Pete ruffled Carl's coily head. They all had a good laugh, and Carl smiled but fell silent.

Marcy mapped out the yard of the old house, and they decided who would bring what and where they would meet up that night. Kevin chimed in that they should all wear black so not to be seen that night and that they could use an old burnt cork on the faces that needed it. Marcy was thrilled at the idea of darkening her face with cork. She'd done it one year when dressing as a hobo for Halloween, and it was fun. "What about flashlights?" Robert mentioned. "There are no streetlights past Miller Street and up toward the woods," he reminded. They all agreed that flashlights would be best. They divided up the lists of things to get and made a pact not to tell anyone of their plan. Marcy hated pacts. It involved everyone spitting on their hands and sealing the deal with a special handshake that seemed to maximize the amount of spit she had to wash off later! It was gross, but a small price to pay to be a part of the group and this Halloween night caper! Just one more sleep and tomorrow was Halloween! She loved that it was on a Saturday this year! There was still plenty to do for Halloween night with trick or treating, parties, finalizing costumes, and now this! They all scurried home to work out the final details of the very busy night ahead.

It was dinner time at the Jackson house. Carl's mother was busy at the stove, putting the finishing touches to dinner as she hummed a soft tune. Carl dropped his books on the buffet beside the pumpkin he had carved the day before. He admired his handiwork as he reached into the wide grin of the orange orb and flicked on the small white tea light. The light flickered briefly then blazed forth an orange light. He knew that a fresh battery would be required for tomorrow night. After all, it would be out on the front step to greet the neighborhood, and it had to look sharp! The house smelled like autumn. The aroma of freshly carved pumpkins, a hearty beef stew, and fresh-baked cornbread wafted through the air. It was the best time of year, Carl decided. Pumpkin lit, he spied the cornbread on the dinner table and reached for a piece. "You better not be touching that cornbread with those dirty hands, mister!" his mother called out without turning around. Carl grinned. His mother knew everything and saw everything much like Marcy now that he thought of it. He wondered if it was just a girl thing, meant to keep guys from having fun. "Yes ma'am," Carl said, and he headed off to the sink to give his hands a good scrub. His mother smoothed a hand lovingly over his head. "Why so late today?" she asked casually, and Carl stiffened at the thought of why he was late. His mother's hand stopped for a brief instant when she felt the slight shift in her son, then continued a second more before picking up the pepper shaker and adding a bit more of it to the stew. "Trouble at school?" she asked. Carl knew that voice. The slight rise in pitch with the question. It was like she already knew. He had to stay cool. "Nah just hanging with the gang at the field. Talking about . . ." He hesitated only a second. "Halloween stuff." He finished as he grabbed a towel to wipe his hands. He busied himself with drying his hands and never looked up. It wasn't exactly a lie, he decided. His mother surveyed him from the corner of her eye. She knew when there was trouble brewing. She put the lid on the stew and turned slowly and arched her brow. "You better not be getting into any trouble like your brothers used to," she warned. "Otherwise, your father will whoop your behind," she added just as her husband strolled through the door. Carl's father was a big man and that, never mind the fact that he was chief of police and had a gun, made him a man not to mess with, and Carl knew it. Carl had seen the trouble his brothers got into when they were younger, and his father was swift to punish them. Carl was the youngest of the three boys and his dad's favorite. His dad was always kind and gentle with them all until someone had stepped out of line. Until now, Carl hadn't even dreamed of stepping out of line.

Carl's dad was still in his uniform from work— his gun and badge already stowed away safely. He smiled at Carl and pulled him in for a hug and to playfully pat Carl's head. What was it about his head that everyone had to touch? Carl thought. "This guy? Trouble?" His dad teased lightly. "Never!" He stated and then just as quickly let Carl go and planted a kiss on his wife's cheek. "Dinner smells wonderful!" he added as he reached for a piece of cornbread. Carl's mom tapped his father's hand before he could grab one. "Don't you dare!" she warned. "Off and wash those hands! You're no different than those boys!" she chided him. Carl smiled at his dad. Perhaps he would get away with this after all!

Soon the whole family had washed and gathered to have dinner. Carl steered clear of the Halloween topic as best he could, and it did not go unnoticed by either of his parents. "What are you doing for Halloween, sport?" His brother Mike was the spitting image of Carl but about a foot taller and 10 years older. Carl kept his eyes on his stew. "Nothing much ... trick or treating with the gang," he mumbled. Carl's parents exchanged a look. It was the kind of look that said, I don't know what you're up to ... but I know it's something. Mike was oblivious to it; his mind was on his date and a party they were going to that night and another the day after that. "Cool ... sounds like fun," he said as he thought of his trick or treating years. Then he added, "Hey ... you gonna ring old lady Cruthers' door this year?" and he laughed. Carl shifted uncomfortably in his seat. "What do I wanna go to that creepy old house for?" he snapped. His brother John was 17 and looked up and laughed. "Carl's too chicken for that stuff," he teased and then made chicken noises that Mike joined in on. "Baaaaak, baak! Baaak! Chicken!" they teased. Carl slouched down lower, his parents taking in the scene with a new sense of interest. "Alright." his mother chimed in. "That's enough. Don't you have a date, Michael?" she reminded. Mike checked his watch and hopped up. "Yeah, I gotta get ready! Thanks for dinner, Mom!" He planted a kiss on his mom's cheek and put his dishes in the sink. "John's turn for dishes!" Mike called out as he sped off taking the stairs up to his room, two at a time. "Hey!" John protested. "I did them" he counted off in his head, "three days ago." His mother advised, "So, it's your turn again." John frowned and got up with his bowl and headed to the sink to reluctantly start the dishes. Carl spooned up the last of his stew and planned to slip off. But not before his mother had given his father a slight nod toward Carl that indicated she wanted him to talk to the boy. "Who are you trick or treating with this year?" Carl's dad asked. Carl was halfway out of the chair but sank back down with the question. *Stay cool*, he said to himself. "Just the guys, well, and Marcy," he said absently. "Uhhmm and where?" his father continued. Carl sat up a little straighter, "Just around here I guess," he said. His father looked at him and then at Carl's mother. He smiled and tapped Carl's nose lightly. "Stay out of trouble," he said lightly. Carl's mother sighed, and his father shrugged at her. Carl looked from one to the other hopeful. "Can I be excused? I have a big math test on Monday," he added "Go on . . . get out of here," his father said with a quick wink. And with that, Carl scrambled off to his room, grabbing his books on the way by. Now all he had to figure out was how to get a big bag of toilet paper out of the house without his parents knowing.

Peter strolled up to his yard, and he could hear them already. His parents, having their nightly fight over, what now? He decided to go in through the back door to avoid all the yelling tonight. It never served him well to walk into the middle of one of the fights as it almost always ended up with his mom yelling even more at his dad because now, they were fighting in front of Peter, and in the end, he would hear her run to her room in tears and cry herself to sleep. He hated it. He wished they'd just get the divorce his father threatened her with all the time. At least all the yelling would be over. The house was small, and unlike Carl's house, it seemed autumn, and Halloween had been forgotten here. It smelled like nothing but laundry when he opened the back door and quietly made his way in, while no one noticed. He grabbed a plain white pillowcase from the laundry basket and opened a cupboard overhead. Rolls of toilet paper, paper towels, and a couple of boxes of Kleenex sat on the dark shelves. He grabbed six rolls of toilet paper and tossed them in the case. That would do him for Halloween night he thought and headed down the dark hall to his dark room the door closing firmly behind him, causing the arguing to stop briefly. He grabbed his ear pods and waited a moment. "Peter? Is that you?" He heard his mother's shaken voice call. "Yeah," Peter called back through the closed door. Her footsteps started down the hall, and Peter stashed the pillowcase under his bed. "Pete, honey? You want some dinner?" She rapped lightly on the door but did not enter. "No, I ate at Carl's tonight, remember?" Peter lied. He knew she never did remember. The fib would account for him being late and would keep him from having to go out there ... where HE was. There was a lull in the conversation as she seemed to be mulling it over. "Oh, right. Okay, I must have forgotten, honey," she said unsurely. "You want to come watch TV then?" she asked. Peter put one earbud in his ear. "No. I've got lots of homework." He lied again. He heard the tell-tale sigh, knowing she had given up on him for the night. "Okay, sweetie but come say good night before you go to bed," she encouraged. He agreed, but they both knew he wouldn't, and he'd be gone in the morning, having grabbed his own breakfast before she would get up. Peter put the other earbud in his ear as his stomach rumbled from a lack of dinner. He'd just wait till his dad stormed out tonight and the house was quiet then go grab something to eat later. It's the way it was every night in the Wilson house. Little did he know that the pattern would change very soon.

Marcy spun the lock dials on the padlock that attached her mint-colored Schwinn to the school bike rack quickly. She was late getting home and was already working up a back story in her mind. Her mother disproved of her friends, said they were a bad influence and that she needed some girlfriends to play with instead of a bunch of boys. "It could only lead to trouble!" her mother would reprimand. Marcy hopped on the bike and headed up the hill toward the stately manor with six bedrooms, five baths, and a swimming pool filled with autumn leaves. The latter of which was a sore spot as her father had not contacted the pool company to cover the pool yet, and it was "well past the season!" her mother would chide. For the most part, her mother would focus her efforts to girlify her sister Pamela. Pamela was five years older than Marcy and had most recently been placed on the list to be groomed for the debutante ball when she turned 16. An honor, that Marcy made very clear to her parents, she wanted nothing to do with. That was a conversation that took her mother all weekend to recuperate from, and Marcy grinned at the memory. But coming in late from school without her parents having known in advance she would be late was rarely tolerated. Marcy rode her bike around the circular driveway twice before heading up the pavers along the side of the house. It was just a thing she liked to do that drove her sister crazy for some reason. The yard was freshly raked, and two huge pristine pumpkins without a single blemish sat on either side of the front door. A faux autumn garland lined the door frame, and a matching wreath hung prominently on the whitewashed door. Marcy rolled her eyes. You could find the look on the front cover of just about every magazine this time of year. The inside wasn't much different. All regal and perfectly positioned. She was only allowed to carve a pumpkin on Halloween day, in the garage, and it had to be thrown out the next morning so they wouldn't get "bugs." "My house, my rules!" her mother would snap if questioned.

Marcy parked her bike in the shed out back and snagged a lawn bag from the shed before heading toward the back door of the main house. It was something her mother would never miss because she never even came out here, never mind doing any gardening or housework. Not that Marcy minded so much because that meant she didn't have to do it either. "Let the maid get that dear" or "the gardener will do that honey" were some of her mother's favorite phrases. She liked that her dad was a bit more helpful where the folks that worked at the house were concerned. They liked her dad; he was kind and polite unlike her mother. As if on cue, "Marcella Justine Wheeler! You get yourself in this house, washed, and at the dinner table immediately!" her mother snapped from the kitchen doorway. Marcella Justine? Wow, so that meant a lecture. Marcy thought to herself. Her mother stood tall and slim in a fall-colored tweed dress with rust-colored shoes to match. Her folded arms ending in long well-manicured cinnamon-colored nails that matched her lipstick. Her salon-colored red hair held tightly in a bun and not for the first time Marcy wondered if that tight bun was the cause for her bitter disposition. As Marcy drew closer, she felt her mother's eyes access her. The jeans, sweater, and… *Oh man! The ball cap!* Marcy muttered under her breath and snatched the cap from her head and shoved it into her backpack quickly. Strawberry blonde hair spilled halfway down her back in beautiful soft curls. She didn't want to lose another ball cap to her mother. She had just broken in this new ball cap! She reached the door, and very quickly pulled the backpack onto her back fully as if to protect it and all its contents. Her mother, satisfied that the girl was following instructions, turned on her heels as Marcy reached the door and headed to the dining room. Marcy sighed inwardly; she had just barely saved another cap!

Marcy was washed and seated for dinner in no time. Their server, Jonathan, winked at her as he placed her napkin on her lap and Marcy grinned. She liked Jonathan; he was a great listener and always gave her good advice when she needed it. It was no secret that her mother resembled an evil queen around here. From what she could gather she had only missed soup and salad and she knew from prior offenses that the meal would move forward, and she would not see either of the dishes. Marcy's mother nodded at Jonathan to serve the next course of the meal then fixed a glare on Marcy that told her that she would be the topic of discussion tonight. "I believe we have discussed on numerous occasions that after-school activities are to be approved by your father and me, have we not, Marcy?" The crisp cool tone matched the season, Marcy thought. "Yes ma'am," Marcy replied with just the right amount of respect and shame that Marcy knew her mother would expect. Marcy looked to her father. A lean tall man with impeccable style. His brown slacks and rust sweater matching her mother perfectly. He had dark brown hair and eyes, the fairest skin she'd ever seen on a man, and well-manicured nails that were blunt on the ends. He winked quickly at Marcy as a sign of solidarity, and Marcy grinned inwardly. Jonathan appeared as if out of nowhere to replace the small sip of water Marcy's mother had taken from her glass, and she barely acknowledged the small act. It annoyed Marcy that her mother disregarded these small acts but was so quick to punish anyone that stepped a hair out of line. "Then what is the reason for being tardy?" Her finely plucked brow rose slightly. Marcy sat up straighter in her chair. "There were some girls in class that asked me about going trick or treating Saturday night." Marcy lied with ease as the truth would see her grounded and potentially in a boarding school. Mrs. Wheeler sat forward in brief excitement then remembering her place sat with her back straight again. Marcy noted she almost smiled as well as her mother caught her father's eye. "Well, this is some pleasant news for once. It's about time you found some girls of your age to make friends with and not that pack of wild boys." She frowned at the word boys then smiled again in a hopeful way. Their meals arrived just then and on a final note of the topic, she added, "I might like to meet these girls" and Marcy left well enough alone for now. "Yes ma'am," she said like a dutiful daughter. Her sister Pamela eyed Marcy suspiciously. She knew she was lying again but would wash her hands of the dreadful girl. Mother would know soon enough—whatever it was she was up to!

Marcy was grateful for one thing about this big old house. At least she had her own room, and it was nowhere near her mother's! After dinner, Marcy begged off to do homework. Her mother was only slightly disappointed to not be able to talk more about these "girls" Marcy met, but Pamela had quickly filled the gap with a conversation about dress colors for next year's ball—a conversation their mother fell right into with great interest. Marcy would never understand the need for a full year to plan such an event but was grateful for the distraction. Marcy had her own planning to do, and once back in her room, she was careful to lock the door behind her. Her room, if she could call it that, was filled with the same kind of gaudy décor the rest of the house suffered from. She'd long since given up on the idea of being able to decorate her own room. If it did not match what her mother wanted, it simply was not allowed or was childish. She made the mistake once of reminding her mother that she was in fact still a child. Her father laughed, but her mother did not. She recalled a long quiet weekend between her parents and a chat with her grandmother about why it was deemed inappropriate to have stated the obvious to her mother. Marcy swung open the white barn-style closet doors and pulled out a small step stool. She hopped up and noted that it would not be long before she didn't need it to reach the top shelf in her closet. She slid a couple of plastic storage tubs filled with sweaters and blankets to one side then reached further back to pull forward a 12" x 6"x 4" wooden box with a small lock on it. She tugged up the necklace she wore under her sweater and on the end was a small key she used to unlock the box. The box was filled with special treasure, like the shell her grandpa gave her before he died and a tiny gold horse that sat atop a small music box that her dad gave her when she was six. She pushed those and many other trinkets aside to extract a plump brown envelop. She opened it, and inside was a stack of bills of money she had saved from birthdays and Christmases. Whenever there was cash in a card, she managed to smuggle part or all of it away before her mother could swoop in and proclaim that it all needed to be put in the bank for college. She wondered how much shaving cream cost and grabbed her phone and typed in the local dollar store URL, then searched for shaving cream. Cheap enough, she thought and slid a couple of bills out of the envelope. She would have plenty of time to get it tomorrow while her mother and Pamela were out shopping for winter clothes. It would be hours before she saw them and all she had to do to get out of it, as usual, was to get up late, take too much time at breakfast, and getting showered and dressed. Patience was not a virtue her mother or sister held! Marcy tucked the bills into the inside pocket of her book bag. She put the box back and carefully concealed it once more. Then she pulled out her Spanish book and workbook and sighed. She could use Kevin about now for this homework!

Kevin arrived home and set his books down. The house was filled with the sights, sounds, and colors of Halloween and *Día de los Muertos*! Pumpkins, skeletons, scarecrows, and sugar skulls were all favorites of his little sisters. Colorful dolls in beautiful skirts were held fast by both girls as he waltzed in and gave kisses to his mother and then to both the girls. His mother smiled, and the girls giggled. "*Llegas tarde hoy?*" His father asked while putting tacos together for the little ones. "English, papa, English!" Kevin reminded his father. They had long ago agreed that they would practice English at dinner time to help his mother, father, and sisters become more fluent in the language. Kevin's sisters were much younger than he was. While they were not twins, the girls looked very much alike. Long black hair with those milk chocolate eyes that the whole family had and chubby little cheeks that glowed rosy red. Rosa was the youngest at two years old and Maya was five now and in her first year of kindergarten, so it was more important now than ever that they practice their English to help the little ones. Kevin knew firsthand how difficult it was to come into his school years and not know much English, and he wanted his sisters to have a better chance at learning English more quickly. "English!" Maya said to her father, and they all laughed. Kevin's mother came to the table with a big bowl of Spanish rice, and the smell was decadent. Kevin sat on the other side of the girls to help Rosa with her dinner. "Hands!" his mother said, and Kevin hopped back up to wash his hands. "Answer your father, English boy!" his mother said. Kevin finished drying his hands and came back to help Rosa just as she was grabbing a spoon of rice. "I'm sorry I was late. I was helping some of my friends and we got to talking about Halloween tomorrow. I lost track of time." There was nothing more important than family to Kevin. He learned the importance of family and heritage at a very early age. His father worked hard as a sales manager for a tech company. Kevin still remembered going with his father to the interview two years ago. At only eight years old, he was helping to interpret for his father, and it got him the job. He also remembered the man hiring his father, pulling Kevin aside and telling him his father was very smart but needed to know more English quickly to keep the job. "You understand?" the man had said to Kevin with great concern. "Yes, sir. I understand. I will teach him." Kevin promised the man and so it was. It was a lot to burden an eight-year-old boy with, but he did what he needed to do for the family and never once complained. Robert would come by from time to time to help as well, and he appreciated it. His father learned quickly but liked to fall back on Spanish anytime he could. Kevin had to remind him that the girls needed to learn too. Rosa wiggled her chubby fingers toward the tortillas. "T-tia! T-tia," she called. Kevin corrected her. "Tortilla, say tor-tilla," he said. Rosa screwed up her face in concentration. "Ta-tia!" Kevin repeated the lesson again. "Say tor," and Rosa mimicked him, "Tor." "Now say tilla," Kevin said. "Tia!" Rosa exclaimed. "Tor-tilla," Kevin said. "Tor-tia!" Rosa shrieked. Kevin grinned and handed her a piece of the tortilla. "Close enough, good job!" he said. His mother beamed with pride. "You will take the girls tomorrow, to get treats?" she asked. Kevin sighed. "No, Momma you promised this year I could go with my friends," he pleaded. There was no way he could bail on his friends, not now. "Yes," she waved at him in understanding. "You take the girls too," she said. "Momma, no!" he turned to his father pleadingly, and his father nodded in understanding. He remembered what it was like to be a young boy and to want to go run free with your friends. "Momma the girls can go with Juan and the family." His father stated and his mother shrugged. "Ok! Ok!" she said, and just like that, the matter was settled. They finished dinner with lots of giggles, and Kevin helped his mother clean the kitchen and later helped put the girls to bed while his father worked on a report. It gave his mother a small break when he was there to help. He spent the rest of the

28

night up in his room working on homework. He was the only boy and was fortunate to have his own room. Just before bed, he pulled out a jar of coins from a hole he had carved behind his nightstand. There wasn't much there but if he went to the dollar store, he'd have enough for a few cans of shaving cream. He had been saving the money for Christmas gifts for the girls and now he would have to find some time to walk the houses up on the hill to see if anyone needed yard work done to replenish the money. He knew Marcy lived up there but never really thought to go to her house. Her mother was tough on everyone who worked for her. He had a cousin whom she fired once because the fire in the fireplace went out too early during a holiday party. "There was not enough wood on the fire! Do I look dressed to add logs to the fire?" she hissed when the girl asked why she didn't add some of the wood sitting next to the fireplace. There was no discussion; she was fired, and that was that. He put the coins in a coin pouch, tucked the jar away, and settled in for the night. He lay awake, wondering what made some people the way they were and eventually fell asleep.

Robert came home, his yard filled to the brim with fall leaves. His mother, sister, and he felt the leaves were too festive to rake and bag; and always left them till after Thanksgiving to dispose of them. There were two well-carved pumpkins in front of the one-story house, and the house was lit up brightly. It was a welcomed sight that he could only think of as home. He walked through the door and dropped his bag into the first room off the hall, his bedroom, then headed toward the back of the house where the smell of pot roast, potatoes, and carrots lured him. "Mom? Patrice?" he called out. "Kitchen!" he heard the two call out in unison. He smiled as he walked into the kitchen to find the two most important people in his life laughing as the table was set and the roast was being pulled from the oven. Patrice looked up and smiled. His sister was a beautiful girl. 16 years old but always at their mom's side to help with the house.

She was five feet three inches, a thin girl with new curves developing and a smile that could win anyone. Patrice was superbly popular at school and co-captain of the cheer team. She was very outgoing, unlike Robert who liked to keep to himself mostly. "Hey, good timing all the work is done!" Patrice joked as Robert walked in. He gave her a quick hug and then his mom. It wasn't lost on him that they were all he had for a family in the world now that his dad was gone. "Hey, little man how is the anime world today?" His mom asked as she set the last of the food on the table. Robert beamed. His mom understood his love of his art. He sat between the two and smiled from one to the other. "Good, Mom, good," he said. No one asked where he'd been, not because they didn't care but because there was always so much to do and little time for questions. "When I go to law school, I am going to look over all your contacts for your artwork and make sure you're getting what you deserve," Patrice stated and winked at him. He nodded and reached for her hand, then his mother's. His sister closed the loop with his mother. Life was good here in their home. They were enough for each other, and they knew it. Robert nodded at his mother. "Momma it's your turn tonight," he said. They all bowed their heads and his mother led them in a simple but meaningful prayer. They were thankful for each other. They ate the delicious meal, and soon Patrice checked her watch. "I promised Mrs. Fleming I would come lock up the shop and clean for her tonight. I figured we could use the extra money," she said humbly. Her mom smiled and nodded. Robert stood quickly; he couldn't work but he could still help around the house. "I'll do the dishes, Momma," he stated. Mrs. Evans smiled brightly. "How did I get such wonderful kids?" she said. Robert felt slightly guilty at the comment. He didn't feel like a wonderful kid. Marcy had stopped him before he left the field and handed him money for eggs for the Halloween prank. Money that his family could use. Life was tough after his dad died. They got by but extra money could go a long way in giving them ALL something they could enjoy. Throwing eggs at a house was a waste and he knew it. But he couldn't back out now. "Patrice isn't all that great," Robert teased. "Hey!" Patrice laughed and grabbed Robert rubbing her knuckles into his head in a noogie. "Hey, you gotta go!" Robert reminded her as he squirmed to break loose, and just as quickly, she let him go. "Yeah, I will see you later tonight, Momma." She promised, and off she went. Robert helped his mother clean up, but she shushed him off early and told him to go work on his sketches. "Momma!" he protested. "No, go on! You're so talented, honey. I'm proud of you." And reluctantly, Robert went off to his room, the $20 bill burning a hole in his conscience.

Halloween had arrived, and just about everyone in town was preparing in some way. Parties were being finalized with shopping lists, decorations, and costumes prepared. RSVPs were called in to party invitations sent days earlier, and every house had bags of candy earmarked for passing out to trick or treaters. Last-minute pumpkins were carved for porch steps to light the way of ghosts, witches, and pirates that would flood the streets in search of loot! The choice belonged to the candy giver. Trick or treat? But everyone knew candy would dissuade the goblins from a trick, or would it? For the one house that never gave treats year after year, it was time to pay the price with tricks. Peter took his bag of toilet paper and stashed it behind the garage. It would be easy to slip out the back door and grab it that night after his parents were asleep. He decided the rest of the day he would spend with Carl and called him up after grabbing some fruit and taking off down the road to the park. "Hey, you wanna hang?" Peter said as Carl answered on the first ring. "What time is it?" Carl asked as he yawned. Pete knew it was early, but he really had nowhere else to go. "I dunno, eight?" Peter offered. Carl was waking up now, and he could sense from his friend's tone that it had been another one of those nights with his parents. "Yeah, just come over. Mom's making pumpkin pancakes," he said.

Peter loved pancakes and rarely got them unless Carl's mom invited him over. "Your mom okay with that?" he asked. Carl's parents knew the situation at Peter's house and were always supportive of Pete joining them last minute for meals and the occasional sleepover. "Yeah, man my parents love you. Get over here!" Carl insisted. Peter smiled. It was nice to hear that someone loved him. He knew his parents did, but they were so wrapped up in themselves he felt like an afterthought. Peter headed over and as always, was welcomed with open arms. "You need anything, Pete?" Carl's father would always offer, and Peter would always politely decline. "Nah, thanks, Mr. Jackson." Then he smiled at Carl's mom. "The pancakes are plenty!" It broke Mrs. Jackson's heart to see Peter going through what was sure to end up in a divorce. She was just glad he had Carl as a friend to help keep him straight and to give him a place to land where people cared. "Peter, you're the only one who truly appreciates my cooking!" his mother teased, and the room erupted in protest. After breakfast, the boys took off to the store to finish up their Halloween costumes for trick or treating later that night. They spent most of the day just hanging out, waiting till dark for trick or treating with the rest of their friends. They knew that this year, trick or treating was secondary to the main event of Ms. Cruthers' house.

Kevin and Robert had decided to meet up at the dollar store to shop for everything they would need for Halloween. Kevin had a list from his mom as well for things the girls needed for that night. Kevin was careful to keep the money his mother gave him, and his change separated. Even though his mother insisted Kevin get himself a treat, he would not use his father's hard-earned money for himself. Kevin sat on the bench outside of the store, watching a black and orange inflatable tube dancer flap endlessly in a random dance used to lure people into the store. He could see down the road what looked like Robert strolling along and what he assumed to be Marcy stopping beside him. Robert hopped up on the seat and Marcy, as she often did, pedaled her bike standing up to give Robert a free ride down to the store. Their cheeks were rosy when they stopped at the bench to greet Kevin. The day was chilly, and a slight wind created a dance of brightly colored leaves all over the town. The three of them grinned wickedly as they entered the store. The store was doing a brisk business with it being both a Saturday and Halloween. Both the registers had queues and shelves were in disarray as shoppers rummaged through them for a bargain. The center aisle was the most popular as it contained Halloween candy, costumes, and decorations. To the right of the store were household and gift items, and the left side had sundries, drug store items, and snacks. Instinctively, they all went straight for the center aisle. They played around, trying on masks, and giggling at the effects of the haunted toys and gadgets. Kevin picked up a make-up kit that had eight basic colors and one cheap foam-tipped applicator. Marcy looked at the big fancy kits. She'd seen Kevin looking at them as well and knew money was tight, so he would get the cheapest kit. She grabbed a fancy kit with more colors, fancy cream pencils, fake tattoos, scar-making clay, and more, then tossed it in her basket. "Hey, I'm getting this for Rosa and Maya!" she exclaimed. "I bet they will have a ball with it." She turned and noted Kevin had put the other kit down. "Is that okay? I love getting them stuff, I don't have a little sister," she said. Kevin gave her a look. "You don't have to buy them stuff," he said. Marcy smiled pleadingly at him. "Come on they are so adorable, and I love spoiling them!" It was true she really did love to see their little faces light up. Kevin gave in with a sigh. "Okay, just this one thing, nothing else!" he warned. Marcy winked at Robert, and they all laughed. They knew Marcy would find something else for them. After a while, Robert nodded to the others to follow him. It was time to buy the things they had come for: shaving cream! They huddled in the aisle a moment waiting for a shopper to move on. "So, what do we say if the cashier asks what we need all of this for?" Robert asked in hushed tones as he added six cans to his basket. Kevin grabbed six more and put them in his basket wondering the same. Marcy's brain was already in high gear, thinking up a story for the cashier. Just then a group of older teenaged girls came into the aisle and grabbed 20 cans of shaving cream. They were laughing loudly and talking about the carnival in the next town over. "I am going to pie Steve so bad at the booth! He will be sorry he signed up!" a girl with long blonde hair was saying. Her stomach was visible from under the crop top and her well-rounded hips fit snugly into a pair of slashed jeans. Robert and Kevin tried not to look, but the girl knew they had and grinned at them. "In your dreams, boys!" She teased and then she winked at Marcy, and she and her friends were gone as quick as they appeared. Marcy's grin spread across her face. "Give me all your stuff." she said to the boys and started to toss everything into her basket. Kevin stared at her then back to the blonde. Robert nudged him. "Close your mouth, man," he said quietly, and Kevin snapped his mouth shut and blushed. With all the items now in her basket and Kevin properly embarrassed, Marcy grinned. "Okay, follow my lead," Marcy said as she tugged off her ball cap, letting her strawberry blonde curls bounce loose down her shoulders. She bent over and flipped her hair back like she'd seen so many girls do, hoping it had some magical effect that would help her. She stood up straight and shook her hair side to side and quickly ran her fingers through it. Kevin stared in awe. He rarely saw Marcy let her hair down, and it looked and smelled really nice. Marcy and Robert looked at Kevin and laughed. "Close your mouth!" they both said and then laughed. "Come on." Marcy said before Kevin could blush again. The boys followed Marcy to the counter, unsure what she was doing. She turned quickly to them when it was her turn. "Just follow my lead," she stressed. Marcy put the items up on the counter and started laughing like that blonde girl and tossed her hair.

"Hey, can you imagine Peter's face when I PIE him at the carnival tonight?" she said loudly and continued to giggle then turned a sharp look on the boys. Robert jumped in quickly, "Oh! Oh yeah he'll be super mad at you!" Robert supplied and nudged Kevin. The cashier rung up the items with super speed and barely even looked up except to ask for cash, which Marcy produced. "Yeah!" Kevin chimed in. "I bet you get him good!" he said. The cashier handed Marcy her change and snapped, "Next!" as she handed the bag over to Marcy. "Thanks!" Marcy said with a sugary sweet voice and tossed her hair again for good measure as they headed off. "Yeah, NEXT!" said the cashier as she looked behind the three of them and waved up the next person to the counter. The three of them made a beeline for the door, and once outside, Marcy burst into laughter as she grabbed her bike, and they headed to the backside of the building to divide up the goods. "Wow! I don't even think she cared!" Marcy laughed and then looked up. The boys were staring at her, and it puzzled her. She held up the bag, "We got it! No questions!" but her smile faded when she realized why they were staring at her. It was the same daffy look they gave that blonde girl. It was her hair. Marcy was annoyed and tugged her ball cap out of her pocket and quickly twirled up the soft creamy hair and jammed it back up into the hat. "Geez! It's just hair!" she snapped at them. Marcy's temper rose as she shifted the ball cap back on her head. She fixed her ponytail, so it hung out the back of the cap once again. Marcy pulled the items from the bags and separated them and then handed them each a bag. They both attempted to hand her their money, and Marcy snapped, "Just keep it!" The boys looked at each other not sure what to do now. "Sorry," Kevin said lamely. Marcy couldn't stay mad at either of them; she nudged him. "Don't be such a guy!" she teased. Robert laughed. "Don't be such a girl!" he retorted, and Marcy shot him a quick glare. "Kidding!" he said, and they all laughed. "Hey, let's drop this off at my shed. I have a good hiding place!" Marcy said. "Yeah, your house is the last one on the way to… well, you know," Robert said glancing around as people walked by. "Good idea!" Kevin said. Since they were all walking together, Robert offered to push Marcy's bike for her. It was something he never offered to do before, but times were changing and so too, Robert noticed, was Marcy.

The streets were teeming with a variety of superheroes, ghosts, vampires, and princesses. Shrieks of laughter and fright filled the night air. It was just past dusk, and the streets were packed with trick or treaters and partygoers! The air was chilly, and the wind was picking up. Leaves created momentary tornadoes that held no power and died out seconds later. Little ones cried in protest when moms forced heavy sweaters over their costumes while older kids ran house to house greedily, grabbing up candy along the way. For many, the night would not end here, there would be parties to go to and dancing to be done and for a small band of five, even later than all the parties, there would be a Halloween visit to Ms. Cruthers' house!

All the bags that they had filled with shaving cream, toilet paper, and eggs were neatly stashed away for later in the night. For now, it was time to cash in on the sweetest time of the year— Halloween! The time when it was expected of them to beg their neighbors for candy! The plan was set, they would start at the lower end of the town and work their way up toward Marcy's and finish up in the hills. Then they would all head home and "go to sleep" and meet up later at midnight on the side of Kevin's house. Kevin's house was in the middle of the rest of them, so it would make a good place to start from. They met at the first house excited to start. Marcy decided to be a baseball player this year. It was quick and easy with little fuss. Robert dressed up as one of his anime characters, in a baggy white shirt, with grey shorts and a blue long-sleeved shirt under it. He completed the outfit with baggy socks and sneakers. "Cool outfit!" Kevin remarked. Kevin went with his grim reaper costume from last year.

It still fit and was good enough to get candy with. Peter and Carl went as pirates this year. They raided Carl's brothers' old costumes after pancakes that morning and, like Marcy, went with what was quick and easy. They marched on from door to door, comparing treats, but as the night grew darker and colder, it was the house on the hill they were all thinking about.

It was finally here, the time for Halloween night to really get started, all the streets were deserted, and house lights were dimmed for the night, as it was well past the time for traditional partier's and trick or treaters to be out and about. Yet in the darkness, there was movement. A handful of slim shadows hovered around a bedroom window. Eager anticipation lit the faces of some, while other eyes shifted about cautiously into the deep dark night; ears tuned into the slightest rustle of a single leaf on the pavement and hearts beat wildly. Nervous excitement and nervous laughter had spread through the group like a virus. "Shhhh... you'll wake the girls!" Kevin said in a harsh whisper to Peter. As agreed, they all wore black pants and a black top to help conceal them within the murky darkness that had long since devoured the daylight. "Well, hurry up! We don't have all night . . . we wanna do this while it's still Halloween." Robert was standing on tiptoes peering into the open window of his friend's first-floor bedroom. He had already smeared blackened cork on the faces of most of the group which left only Kevin to contend with. He was proud of himself—having come up with the outfits and the use of the burnt cork to ensure they were well concealed, but he supposed that was the artist in him. They were clever outfits and surely no one would see them or see them well enough to identify them at any rate. "Alright, alright." Kevin tied off the laces of his sneakers quickly and grabbed his flashlight and pillowcase from the floor. The items in the pillowcase clinked together noisily when he lifted it. "Shhhhh!" Robert hushed him. "That's all we need is for your parents to catch us and find out we're going to this creepy place! Man, you're lucky I'm even going," Robert said as he took the bag from his friend's hand, so Kevin could make the final leap from his bedroom window. They joined their other three friends. Kevin snatched up the bag again and snickered at Robert while his friend smeared the last of the burnt cork all over Kevin's face. "What's the matter, Bobby? You scared?" he teased loudly so the others would hear. Robert straightened up and glanced around at the taunting grins of his friends. "No I am not scared! I just have better things to do than rattling some old bat's cage!" He retorted and strode off purposefully toward the road that led to Ms. Cruthers' home, tossing the spent blackened cork remains to the ground. The others stood there staring after him. Robert sighed inwardly. There was no use letting them think he was scared; otherwise, they would tease him all night. The truth was his heart wasn't in it. How disappointed his mom and sister would be if he got caught. But he couldn't let everyone down; he knew he was a big part of why they were out here. With that in mind, he turned quickly with a grin on his face. "Well? Come on! Unless YOU'RE scared!" he laughed in a convincing manner and led them all out toward the road. The others fell quickly in stride, none of them wanting to appear slow to join the mission at hand as that would only show weakness in this crowd. For they all knew that on a night like All Hallow's Eve when your imagination was filled with wild possibilities, it was not the time to show weakness of any sort! The consequences could be your undoing!

They walked on shoving each other from time to time as they joked quietly. The last thing they wanted was to be too loud and wake someone in the neighborhood. Never once did they realize that they were being followed. It happened so quietly and smoothly in almost an instant as if on some magical cue, something quietly rose from the shadows. It was small and ever so quiet as it began to track the kids from a distance like a shadow in the night. It was quieter than a leaf blowing through the air, yet as quick as the blink of an eye which allowed it to be elusive as it followed them on their journey. They marched on, but they soon noticed that the closer they got to that old lady's house, the quieter each of them became. Instinctively, the group began to huddle a little closer. They weren't quite certain if it was because of how close they were to the old house or something else. Unknown to them, something else had emerged from the shadows and continued to keep pace with them just far enough away so it would not be noticed.

It seemed the closer they got the darker and colder the night became. The wind whistled louder through the trees. None of them would ever recall the exact moment it happened but a foreboding silence fell upon them all. They marched a little slower in their silence, sneakers trampling leaves as they moved along the deserted street toward the darkened house on the hill. It was Kevin who showed the first signs of panic. He felt a trickle of fear creep up his neck as if the wind was whispering eerie secrets only to him. He glanced back once then twice to check behind them because all his instincts told him that they were being followed. A bead of sweat broke loose from his neck and trickled in a slow thin line down his back. His senses went into overdrive, and he could not be sure anymore if he was just being paranoid or if it meant something more. He did not dare speak out of fear; the others would tease him horribly if it were nothing. But the nagging feeling remained, and his heartbeat quickened at the slightest sound. They trudged along but no longer at the exciting pace they had started the journey with. Now the pace became a foreboding crawl, and they held tightly together moving almost as one. Kevin could not help but wonder if the others were feeling the same way he was or if they had all just slowed down after the long day of Halloween parties and trick or treating.

Robert was the next to sense the chilling feeling that they were being watched, and he too looked about but saw and heard nothing.

"Hey" whispered Marcy. "You guys hear something?" They all stopped immediately and automatically pulled closer together. They looked at each other and then deep into the night around them. The wind whispered through the trees and leaves scraped past them along the pavement as if to warn them to turn back. Their ears all tuned into the sounds of the night yet all they heard was the quick heavy beat of their own hearts and the shallow breathing of each other. "Come on it's nothing," said Peter. "No wait!" hushed Kevin. He could feel his heart beating hard in his ears and more and more beads of sweat formed and trickled more rapidly down his back. "I heard something too …" "Yeah," said Robert. He had decided that since Kevin was brave enough to admit it, now would be the time for him to chime in too. "I think some-one's following us." Peter grinned wildly. He was the kind of boy who seemed fearless and thrilled at the chance to tease the others. "You girls wouldn't be SCARED, now, would you?" He laughed at them, and a snide grin came to his lips. It was then that they all heard the crush of leaves behind them, and they all stood frozen in the darkness of the night. It was a fear like nothing they had felt before. It was as if they were frozen in time and unable to move from what could, at any moment, lunge from the darkness at them. There were no houses nearby to run to, just an empty field to one side and the deep dark woods just ahead of them on the opposite side of the road. Those woods, thought Kevin, that was where the noises came from, and he knew it. It wasn't deep in the wood either; it was close, too close for his comfort. But was it close enough to reach out to them and touch them? Robert saw his own fear mirrored in Kevin's eyes and was not interested in finding out if whatever they heard was in striking distance. "Come on" he urged the others to follow him to the other side of the road along the field. Kevin and Marcy both followed quickly. Peter stood there, hands on his hips, and snickered at them. "You can't be serious," he retorted. "Come on, let's go ghost hunt-ing!" he nodded his head toward Carl and tugged on his jacket.

Carl stood in the middle of the road between the two sides, deciding who to join: Peter or the others. Peter was frustrated and waved a hand in dismissal at them all. Maybe it was better if he just took off on his own, he thought. "Aww, go on then! Go join the girls and visit grandma. I'm going to check this out." And with that, Peter headed off into the deep dark woods... alone. Carl moved quickly to catch up and join the others. "He's just itching for a fight that one" he motioned to Peter as they all watched Peter disappear into the woods with his flashlight. "He's been like that ever since his dog disappeared up here a week ago," Carl stated matter-of-factly as he reached the others, and they continued to move on. Carl had always been a quiet boy of sound reasoning and never believed in fearful things. He always loved the intrigue and the pursuit of the mysterious if for no other purpose than to reason out the logic of it all. The others stared at him, the reminder of Pete's dog going missing put a whole new spin on things, and a slight hint of panic began to weave its way through the minds of them all, even Carl. "That's probably why he took off. He probably thinks it's his dog and went to see," said Carl as he began to set the pace again toward their original destination. "You mean they never found his dog, Sam?" Marcy asked nervously. Carl shook his head and proceeded to rationalize it more for himself than the others. "Nah... maybe ran off in the woods and a wolf got it. He never had a collar on, he could have gotten picked up by someone thinking he was a stray and they kept him or something. I think Peter is more inter-ested in looking for old Sam than old lady Cruthers." He shrugged as if it all was perfectly logical, and they all looked at the house looming ahead of them. Its foreboding form sitting eerily on the hill, beckoning them to come forth into its darkest depths. They were nearly there. "Or something" Robert mumble looking at the others.

Kevin nodded his head toward the group and then to the house to suggest they all follow him. This was an adventure like nothing they had done before and leaving his foolish friend Peter behind him, he felt a sudden surge of bravery building up inside him again. It gave him a new sense of courage to continue the journey. "Come on, this is the coolest thing we've ever done, his loss!" He started again, and the others followed silently behind. Only once did Carl glance back to the spot they left their friend. It was reasonable, he thought to himself, that Peter would want to have a look around for his old dog. He was sure the noise they all heard was nothing more than a fallen branch or a squirrel scurrying about for food. The fact was that Peter was gone having disappeared into the woods and no one mentioned it again. Nor did anyone mention that they each had the feeling they were *still* being followed by someone or something. In the back of their minds, each of them had the sneaking suspicion that it was probably Peter trying to scare them and that alone boosted their need to be brave and move on. It would be just like Peter to jump out at them, thought Marcy, and she kept a watchful eye for him.

They were close to the house now, and they ducked stealthily behind a row of shrubs. Their hearts beating wildly at the reckless-ness of their plans. They had all been friends for at least the last four years, some of them for more, and this was by far the wildest thing they have ever gone through with. Eyes glimmered with mischief, and wicked grins spread across all their faces as they glanced at one another. They made it. They were here! They whispered as they reviewed their plans to terrorize the old woman that lived within the wretched old house. She kept the town in fear, year after year, and it was their turn now to return the scare! They all synchronized their watches. Kevin handed out the flashlights from his bag to each of them, and they all quietly slipped off one by one around the perimeter of the dark property to get in place just like Marcy had mapped out for them. Once separated, they were more keenly aware of every sound the night wind whispered to them, and even in the coolness of the night, beads of sweat pierced their brows. They never accounted for the fear of what being alone and separated would be like. Every leaf that fluttered by was deafening, and the night wind whispered her secrets more loudly now. They could hear its warnings beware... danger... the wind moaned. They squatted in their positions both fear and excitement filled them. All were ready, all eyes staring into the darkness toward the house; their Halloween night caper had begun in earnest! How often had they joked that not even a starved mouse would dare step foot on this property? Yet here they were, doing the unthinkable. Their imaginations ran wild with thoughts of the old woman catching them and whispering grim, magical incantations in strange tongues to each of them, and it struck even more fear into their hearts.

Kevin glanced nervously at this watch; it was only five minutes till midnight. He looked over to where Marcy was to be stationed, but he could not see her. Was it just the darkness? Was she gone? It was much darker than the road they had traveled to get here. The only light they had was the dim light of the moon, which hid behind darkened clouds most of the night. It was too risky to shine his flashlight over to where she should be. It didn't help that a swift-moving fog was settling in as well. It was as if the fog was beginning to seep in all around them now that they had been lured in closer to the house. The haunting whispers of the secrets that lie within taunted him. Kevin was relieved that he could still see Carl and Robert moving into place and breathed a small sigh of relief. He reminded himself that they were all in this together, they had a pact! Kevin snickered inwardly at the thought that Marcy had probably just chickened out. Girls! He laughed to himself. He tried to reassure himself of this, but his mind wandered to the unspeakable things that could happen if any of them were caught by the old witch. Yes, he thought nervously, that's what he would tell himself Marcy had run home … just scared that's all.

It was exactly midnight now and the faintest whistle drifted through the air and slowly Carl took the first steps toward the house then Robert then Kevin. But still, there was no Marcy. Kevin felt a chill run up his spine as if he were being watched by something in the dark. "Marcy?" he whispered desperately. Perhaps she was pulling some lame prank on him. But the only reply was the wind whistling through the trees. This was no time for games, and the others were counting on him, so he moved on. He was right up next to one of the huge dark windows, and he dropped below it and dug through his bag extracting a large can of shaving cream. He flicked off the top grinning wildly at the thought of slathering this all over the windows of this creepy old house. He began to rise to start the deed. "This will teach you... you old bat!" he whispered. His finger poised over the button and as the first rush of air began to escape from the can, he felt something grab him from behind. The can thumped to the ground—the splash of shaving cream barely reaching the window as a cold clammy hand cupped his mouth before a single sound could be uttered. The last thing he remembered was being dragged by something of superhuman strength backward into the dark as his world spun wildly, and everything went black. He had passed out cold!

Carl had reached the side of the house where the trees stood barren and lifeless. They seemed to reach for him in the darkness as he crept by. His bag was filled with soft white rolls of toilet paper intended for those same trees. He dropped and rolled with the bag behind a large rock, reaching into the bag. He was prepared for that faint whistle that would tell him to begin. He couldn't see Kevin or Marcy, but he quickly reasoned that he wouldn't as they were now on the other side of the house. He could just barely see the shadow of Robert in the distance and watched as the figure emitted a soft low whistle into the wind that carried softly to him. It was time! As Carl stood up fully, his arm flew up and hurled the first roll of toilet paper into the night air toward the first lanky tree that held barely a dozen dried up leaves in its darkened branches. As it flew through the crisp night sky in slow motion, the powder white paper caught onto a twisted branch, spilling the remaining contents of the roll down like snow on the darkest of nights. It was magical, and he grinned in awe of his handiwork and reached for another roll to continue his midnight artistry. Roll after roll cascaded through the air in a silent symphony only a kid could truly enjoy. He took a moment to admire how the soft white paper billowed in the breeze just as the moon peeked out from behind the clouds. It was the most beautiful thing he had ever seen! Carl was enjoying himself… for now.

By the front door, a final figure of Robert had arrived; he was very careful with his bag for the contents were quite delicate and his was the most important job. Robert rested the bag at his feet gently and looked to his watch. One minute, and he would give the signal. He reached into the bag and extracted a couple of long narrow flimsy cardboard boxes and lined them up at his feet quickly but carefully. He wondered briefly if the sound of cracking eggs against the ancient web-covered door would wake the evil that lurked within. He glanced at his watch… it was time. Fingers to the lips, he let out the low whistle just as he had practiced it the night before in his backyard. Marcy said he was the best whistler in the group, so it was left to him to start the mission for all. His chest filled, and he expelled a low soft whistle that on its own seemed normal but in the night air with the wind to accompany him, seemed much eerier than he anticipated, and a shiver went up his spine. It was time! The plan was they would all do their part and run back down the hill to the old oak on the edge of the road to meet up. Excitement got the better of him, and he reached greedily for one of the cartons, tore open the lid, and stared at the contents as though he had never seen eggs before. At that moment, the moon slipped from behind the clouds, and the eggs took on an eerie bluish-white hue... it was almost magical. He was filled with excitement for a thing he had never dared to do in his life before. Holding the carton in one hand, he reached for the eggs. Suddenly, he heard the snap of a twig, and he froze with one hand hovering inches above the eggs. His head twisted right... there was nothing there. He turned left and fear struck him as a large dark figure moved quickly and quietly toward him. The last thing he heard was the carton falling on top of the sack and the sound of dozens of eggs cracking against the concrete pavement they came to rest upon. The sound echoed in his ears as the darkness enveloped him and in moments he was gone.

Carl continued to dance around the trees as roll after roll of soft white paper was tossed high into the air, cascading down over the dark lifeless trees. It somehow made him feel fearless as though the white of the paper cast a magical light into the darkness of the night. He turned toward the house to marvel at all his handiwork and as he did a solitary light flickered to life high above him in the third-floor window. It was not a bright light. It cast a dim yellow murky half glow against the dingy pane it shone through. As if on cue, the moon slipped quietly behind the dark clouds, and Carl wondered if even the moon feared Ms. Cruthers! Carl stood frozen on the spot as if her magic held him frozen in place like the roots of the trees beside him. His mind spun wildly as a black form slowly appeared in the window and stared down at him from high above those darkened grounds where the dim light now flickered once, then twice. He knew instantly it was the old woman! His heart was beating franticly as the thin wiry figure glared down at him, her long boney finger pointed directly at him as it shook wildly! He could almost feel that boney hand upon him, and fear shot through him. She was cursing him! He just knew it! The old woman *was* a witch, and she was casting some devilish spell that would do unspeakable things to them all! He had to run... the bag was nearly empty, and he dropped it.

Finding every ounce of courage, he began to run as fast as he could away from the house, the old witch, and the torture they were sure to endure if caught! His heart racing and blood pounding in his ears he thought only to escape but, at that moment, called out to his friends to warn them. "Come on! RUN!" he yelled to the others, but no one joined him. He stumbled only once... and dared not look back to see if the others were coming. He knew if they had not joined him yet, they were doomed to face the wrath of the town's witch! He ran and ran until he was far from the house and back on the roadside behind the bushes near the oak tree and nearly out of breath. He looked back but there was no sign of his friends. He bent over taking deep breaths. His lungs stung as he tried to calm himself. "She's... she's got them all..." he whispered through fear-stricken gasps. "She... got them all..." he repeated with his hands on his knees still trying to catch his breath. He heard the scuff of shoes and snapped up straight ready to run again. "Almost all!" He heard a voice boom and a hand reach out toward him. He screamed "Ahhh..." and jumped backward, losing his footing, and landing squarely on his backside. But wait... this was a voice he knew and recognized and most of all trusted and relied upon. "DAD! Aww man... I am glad to see you!" He accepted his father's rough calloused hand and rose, brushing off his jeans. He was still in a state of panic and said, "She's got them all! Kev, Marcy, Rob... they're trapped... in the house; I just know it!" His eyes wild and pleading as words came quickly between ragged breaths. "She... she tried to curse me... and..." Carl's father stood listening and trying not to grin at his son. It took a lot to spook his son to the point that he lost all reason. His son stared up at him his wild expression turning to one of dismay. "Well? Aren't you going to arrest her or something? I mean... you're the police!" Carl stated impatiently. Carl felt he'd reasoned this out. He had the facts... he had seen it all with his own eyes, hadn't he? "Let's go," his father stated calmly. "I have something to show you." he added. Carl followed his father as he headed back toward the far side of the house. He could feel the rise of panic well up within him. "Dad? We're not going back up there without back up or something... are we?" Carl whispered in a panic as he tugged frantically at his father's jacket. As much as he admired his dad, he was feeling a bit like he needed more than just his dad to combat this one. "Yes, I am and so are you," his father stated flatly. "But Dad..." Carl began. "No buts... move it," his father said as he firmly grabbed Carl by the biceps and moved him along. They reached the edge of the property, and the whole house was lit up now. It was not quite so foreboding as it had seemed in the dark of the night. But still, Carl knew what she'd done, hadn't he seen it? A flicker of doubt crossed his mind as they got closer. Carl could see his father's police car just on the other side of another set of shrubs, and there were figures inside it. His father motioned to the other officer standing by to open the door to the car. "Come on kids... you have some apologizing to do." From the back seat of the vehicle, out stepped his three friends: Kevin, Robert, and Marcy. A swell of relief poured through Carl. The three of them all held their heads low and mumbled "Yes, sir," in unison and shuffled toward Carl and his father. His father pointed to the house, and the three of them headed toward it. Carl stared at them all in disbelief. "Wait... you can't be serious! I'm not going back up there!" The others stopped and looked back, hopeful that they may avoid the same. Carl's father's face grew stern. "Oh yes you are, and you are going to knock on the door as well," he stated bluntly and pointed toward the door purposefully. "GO," he demanded, and they all fell in line and marched to the front door of the house.

Carl looked back at his father, and his father nodded once, indicating he should knock. Carl raised a fist slowly to the door, and as he was about to knock, the door creaked open slowly. Carl backed up slamming into the rock-solid figure of his father. Fear gripped him, and he wondered why the rest of his friends didn't simply run for their lives! The old woman met his father's eyes with a smile. Carl was amazed at what he saw... she was not at all the dreadful-looking creature everyone had described her to be. She almost seemed like a sweet-looking old woman. She wore a white robe with pink slippers to boot! "Officer! Thank you for coming so quickly!" she cooed with relief. "Good evening, Ms. Cruthers... I have a couple of kids from town who just could not wait till morning to meet you. They have something to tell you. Kids?" They all looked up sheepishly and apologized for trying to frighten her and for the mess they had made of her porch and trees. Carl included. "You know," she began softly, "it wasn't too many years ago another young man and his friends tried the same thing when my grandmother lived here!" She winked at Carl's father. "In fact," she added, "I shall tell all of you the story when you come back tomorrow." She finished. They all stared up at Carl's father pleadingly. "Yes, you heard Ms. Cruthers, you will all come back tomorrow to set things right here. And, as an added favor, you will tidy up ALL of the grounds for Ms. Cruthers." They all bowed their heads in shame at how they had treated Ms. Cruthers. It seemed she was not quite the wicked old witch they thought her to be. "Yes, sir," they all said in unison. "But wait, where is Peter?" Carl suddenly remembered they had parted ways in the woods. "Peter?" his father asked. "We didn't see Peter when we came up to collect all of you." Carl told his father what had happened, and after bringing the other kids home, Carl's father sent out a small search party to look for Peter in the wooded area. While the search party looked for him, Carl's father went to Peter's home only to find that he had never arrived at home that night either. In fact, the house was completely empty. It appeared that someone had moved out in a hurry.

The next morning came early. Carl and his father rounded up the other kids. It had been too late to bring them all home, so they all slept on the living room floor in sleeping bags at Carl's house. Carl's mother was calling their parents to let them know their kids were all safe at her home. Kevin's and Robert's parents were much more forgiving of their boys than Marcy's father was of Marcy. Mrs. Jackson specifically asked for her father, knowing full well that if she gave the news to Marcy's mother, the conversation would have been much worse. As it was her father was going to cover for Marcy, and he would deal with her mother when they got home. Marcy wiped at a tear when Mrs. Jackson gave each of them the news of what their parents had to say. Robert gave Marcy a consoling hug. "It'll be okay," he whispered. "At least it wasn't your mom, right?" And Marcy nodded silently and stifled further tears. "I'm very disappointed in all of you. Now wash up, and I want you all in my kitchen in five minutes. Do you understand me?" Mrs. Jackson was scarier than her husband when she was angry, and they all nodded and ran for the bathroom to wash up. Three minutes later, the four of them came to a screeching halt in the kitchen doorway. Carl's brothers were standing along the wall with grins on their faces. Michael was making a "tsk, tsk" noise at Carl. On the other side of the room were Robert's mother, Kevin's father, and Marcy's dad. None of them looked as amused as Michael and John. Mrs. Jackson strode in from the pantry with coffee for everyone, and the parents sat while their children stood in silence. Mr. Jackson came in with his full uniform on, his gun at his side and his badge polished and sitting on the table. He was taking time out of his morning to deal with the matter, and Carl knew that did not make him happy. Carl looked from him to his mother and decided his mother was still scarier. "Oooooh, Carl... you're in trouble!" came the low chuckle, and as soon as it was out, Mrs. Jackson whipped around. "You two, OUT!" she said to her two older sons. John's mouth gaped open. "But I didn't..." "OUT!" she snapped, and the two boys made haste upstairs. They would listen in from the stairwell.

Mr. Jackson stifled a grin then turned to the kids with his best police chief face. "You WILL..." he began, "apologize to your parents for making them worry about you and for your incredibly poor judgment." He stated. Marcy Carl, Kevin, and Robert exchanged looks of confusion with each other as they were not sure who should speak first. "NOW!" Mr. Jackson clarified. The kids all jumped. Now it was Marcy's dad that stifled a grin. All at the same time, the kids apologized to their parents. It wasn't quite what he intended, but Mr. Jackson let them go on. It was a bit comical, but the parents all decided the "scared straight" method would be best here. When they finished, he continued, "You will now apologize to MY WIFE for me having to wake her up at 3 a.m. to accommodate you all so as not to wake your families." Marcy, Kevin, and Robert all apologized to Mrs. Jackson. When they were done, Carl looked over at his mom and said, "Mom, thanks for taking care of my friends last night," and very quietly looked back to his dad. Mrs. Jackson put a hand to her chest and took a deep breath. Now *this* was the sweet Carl she knew. His dad gave a flash of a wink to Carl and continued, "You will ALL be picked up at 1 p.m. today by one of the city trucks, and you will spend the afternoon cleaning up the mess you made of Ms. Cruthers' yard. Furthermore, you will all, *with feeling*, apologize to Ms. Cruthers for your unneighborly conduct. Are we clear?" Mr. Jackson looked to each one, and they all nodded. "Until then, you will return home with your parent for whatever additional punishment you have coming to you. You are dismissed, except you." He pointed at Carl. "You will be driven to and from school for the next week. You will hand me your cell phone now please." Carl handed over his phone immediately without question. "You will not use the house line, and there will be no TV. Every night will be your turn for dishes for the rest of the week. Understood?" His father's voice was a bit softer but still quite firm. "Yes sir," Carl said. Carl could hear his brother Michael just loudly enough say "Yes!" when he realized he was getting out of dishes for the week. Robert's mother held her son's chin in her hand and surveyed his face. "I'm very disappointed in you," she said softly and then guided him by his shoulder out the door after thanking the Jacksons. For Robert, it was the most crushing thing she could say to him. She didn't punish him in the typical sense like Carl was punished. She only took his sketch pad and pencils for the week that Carl was being grounded. It was enough, and she knew it. Kevin's dad said nothing as they walked out except to thank Mr. Jackson for bringing his boy home. When they got in the car, Mr. Rodrigues reached over and ruffled Kevin's hair. "Was she as crazy as they say, *hijo*?" He asked. Kevin looked at his dad and the grin on his face. "Dad?" Kevin said. He thought for sure he would be in trouble. His father started the car and looked over at Kevin. "You make sure you tell your mother I yelled at you a lot!" he warned, and Kevin smiled at him. "I'll never do this again, Papa," Kevin said quietly. His father winked at him. "I know," he said simply. The last to leave was Marcy and her father. Her father nodded to Mr. Jackson and then Mrs. Jackson. Marcy went quietly to the car. The ride home was silent. When they pulled into the driveway, they sat in the car, neither of them got out. Her father stared forward as he spoke. "I would have thought," he began in a quiet disappointed tone, "after watching how your mother treats the staff and others in our community, that *you*, of all people, would have been kinder than this." Tears rolled down Marcy's face. "I'm sorry, Dad. We were just being stupid kids... I'll make it right." Marcy sniffed. He looked at her and truly believed she would. He patted her hand lightly. "See that you do. You're not this person," he said and then got out of the car leaving her there to collect herself before she came inside.

Later that afternoon, they all went to Ms. Cruthers' house. They cleaned up after their Halloween prank and raked and tidied her entire property till not a single leaf remained on the ground. They were all amazed to see the tiny garden she had in the backyard. It was full of beautiful flowers and NOT rotten old weeds like the stories they heard in the school halls! It turned out it was all she could do at her age to keep the small garden, so the rest of the yard had become unkempt over the years. Her home was tidy and the cakes and lemonade she served them later were delightful. She told them all the story of when Carl's father and his friends tried a similar prank on her grandmother, and they all had a good laugh. Carl looked over at his dad, and his father winked at him. At that moment, Carl knew things were not as bleak as he thought and brighter days were coming. Back when her husband was still alive, she recanted, he would have given them all a good whooping had he been allowed! She recalled the story with a touch of sorrow as her grandmother and husband were long since gone now. They could see the fond memories flicker through her eyes at the mention of her husband. She smiled sweetly at them all, and they realized she was quite a nice old woman after all. They felt bad for their behavior and for believing all the stories about her. They offered to stop by from time to time and tidy her yard for her. She smiled but politely declined their offer. She told them she preferred her solitude, and soon enough she sent them all on their way.

That week at school everyone was talking about the Halloween night caper that happened and Marcy, Robert, Kevin, and Carl were all quizzed about what happened and what it was like, but they kept quiet about it all. They never felt it was something to brag about and mostly just whispered amongst themselves about what could have happened to Peter and his mom. No one seemed to know, not even Carl's dad. After a couple of days, the kids at school gave up asking about it and things went back to normal. Carl asked his dad from time to time about Peter, but he never did talk to Carl about it and eventually, he stopped asking. A few years later, Ms. Cruthers passed on. They were all 16 and 17 when they heard the news.

"Hey..." Kevin called out to Marcy and Robert who were yet again kissing on the bleachers. They looked over to Kevin. "*Hola mi amigo!*" Robert called to him. "*Hola!*" called Marcy. Kevin smiled. He liked how they would randomly use Spanish now and how good they were in it! "I was talking to Carl; his dad says Ms. Cruthers passed on last night up at the hospital." Kevin dropped onto the bench next to them. It was a beautiful fall day, and the sun was shining brightly on them. Marcy's strawberry blonde curls shone beautifully as she turned. "No way... last night?" she said. Robert thought a moment then his eyes lit up. "Come on! On Halloween night?" he said with disbelief. Kevin laughed. "True story... I looked it up on my phone when he told me," Kevin replied as he nodded with a grin. "Wow," Marcy said softly. "Do you think she was..." Robert raised a brow at his girlfriend. "Oh no... not that again. We are not..." He raised his hands in the air, and Marcy and Kevin laughed. "Hey," Kevin said quietly. "Let's go pay our respects. What do you say?" Marcy and Robert smiled. "Yeah, I think we should," Marcy said, and Robert agreed. Later that week, the four of them went together to pay their respects to old Ms. Cruthers. They went in together and stood silently, each saying a prayer for the sweet old woman. As they walked away, a tall thin blonde guy with vivid blue eyes in a black suit walked up to them. "Room for one more?" he asked. "Pete!" Carl exclaimed and was shushed by a woman close by. They went out to the parking lot amidst the rush of fall leaves; the wind whipped around them as they stepped out. They all hugged. "Where were you? What happened?" Carl began. "How did you know about this?" Marcy asked as she pointed to the funeral home. Peter laughed. "I told your dad not to tell you I was coming. He called to let me know. Besides, it was time I came back," Peter said. Peter told them all the story of how he came home, and his mom had them packed and told him she was leaving his dad. Things were rough for a while, and they were in protective custody. As it turned out, his dad was doing more than just yelling at his mom and Peter never knew because he was never around and was too young to really understand it all. "What about your dog?" Kevin asked. He told them how his mom had given his dog to his aunt to keep safe and he was back with him now. He went on to say how his mom remarried six months ago, and they decided to move two towns over. He kept meaning to stop in, but he had a younger sister, Melissa, and a little brother, Henry, now, and things were busy with the new family and new school. He said he ran into Carl's dad a couple of days ago and they exchanged numbers and then he got the call yesterday about Ms. Cruthers. "Wow, so how long are you here for? Can you stay overnight?" Carl asked. Peter laughed. "I'm like an hour away man. I can come by anytime." Peter pointed to a creamy white sports car and clicked a fob, and the lights on the car flashed and bleeped. "WHAT?" Marcy shrieked, and they all went over to check out the car. "Yeah, my stepdad got it for me for my birthday this year . . . said a kid my age needed a car." Pete smiled but not so much because he got a car, more for the fact he had a stepdad that cared about him, and his mom was safe. Carl patted Pete on the back. He was happy for him. He could see a change in his friend for the better, and it made him happy. "Man . . . it's good to see you again." Carl nodded toward Robert and Marcy. Marcy's hair flowing in the light breeze. She wore a pretty, green dress with pale pink flowers and a pair of black Mary Janes. She and Robert were holding hands and grinning while Kevin checked out the car. "You believe those two?" He shook his head looking at how in love Robert and Marcy were. Peter laughed and bumped Carl playfully on the shoulder. "You're too slow my friend, just too slow!" And they headed over to join the others. He wasn't wrong, Carl thought. But he always thought Marcy and Robert would end up together.

As the years passed, they let the mysteries of the old woman on the hill die with her. Many a schoolchild would still whisper in the hall's years later about the Halloween night caper, and the story would always change as children would make up new events where they could not remember what truly happened. And so, it was that Ms. Cruthers' legend lived on for many, many years. As they grew and had their own families, Robert and Marcy; Kevin, Peter, Carl, and their wives would share the stories with their own children. On every Halloween night after all the day's events were over, they would dim all the lights for a final bedtime story of the Halloween night caper! Some said the old woman's spirit still wandered the streets late on Halloween night looking for stray children still out of bed! Others told their kids the real story of what happened. A part of them rested easy at having met the old woman and finding her to be just a lonely but kind old woman. Another part of them always wondered if she really was a witch and had planned to join the spirit world on Halloween night and really was watching over the town each Halloween looking for mischievous kids.